VOLCANO GIRL

Written By: JD Wilson

Illustrated By: Ethan Roffler

This story is made possible by Stories Untold, a company dedicated to bringing stories to life for the world to read.

The typeface Colby CpExLit created by Jason Vandenberg.

1

For Becky...And Beck

A legend is born a story that just needs time to grow.
Like the legend about the girl, who came from the volcano.

3

Once upon a heartbeat, or perhaps that silence in between,
Hear the murmur within a mountain; This is where we set our scene.

If you climb down to rock bottom,
a shady village you will find;
This place that posts no vacancies,
for positivity of any kind.

In this far-off frozen village, there lived a troubled tribe.
Some say that they gave off an angry Pennsylvanian sort of vibe.
There was no official name for this tribe of below averages.
Rumor has it, they called themselves "The Savages".

While each "Savage" villager was no different than you and I, there was one distinction, barely visible to the eye.

Although everyone was made of flesh and bone, somehow over time, their hearts had turned to stone.

They were a melting pot of pessimism, filled with hate and rage.
First banning the book of love, then burning every page.

Perhaps it was the depressing weather that dampened their attitudes.
Most of the cold-hearted "Savages" displayed such miserable moods.

The children just hid inside, and bickered all day long.
They wasted playtime screaming about who was right or wrong.

Game days turned to fight nights. This call-out culture loved missed calls.

Where children swing for the fences, while elders argue over walls.

The only laughter heard from this tribe seemed to be at others expenses.
Would anyone in this hateful village ever come to their senses?

Then on the coldest of days, or so the story goes,
the ground broke away and, "KABOOM"...
From the soil a volcano arose!

The Savages stood in astonishment, standing at the volcanic base;
A glazed look of wonder, upon each jaw-dropped face.

"A miracle! It's a miracle!", yelled a Savage to the snow-filled skies.
The children thunderously agreed, at the magnificent sight before their eyes.

The elders, however, had something else to say,
"This volcano is no miracle, but rather it's a curse! We must block it
off and stay away; It could make things far worse!"

The elders began to form a plan, and they chose one rather abrupt,
"If we pretend the volcano is not there, then perhaps it won't erupt!"

Maybe they were just too scared, and confused in the bitter cold.
They decided to ignore the volcano, heading back to their arctic abodes.

Time passed in the wintry village; Soon memory of the volcano faded.

Eventually, those stubborn old Savages, resumed
their lives so jaded.

Children continued fighting, whining for the win.
Elders went on complaining, as if kindness was a sin!

Then one chilly afternoon, the volcano began
billowing puffs of smoke;

Followed by a thunderous rumbling,
to which the Savages all awoke!

19

A shadowy figure emerged through the smog-like swirl;

She would be known from then on as Volcano Girl!

20

She couldn't have been taller than maybe four foot three, yet, from the top
of the volcano, she seemed tall as tall could be.

Volcano Girl had straight long hair, that flowed down to her knees;
Slowly waving back and forth, from the obsidian breeze.

Shining from where her heart should
reside, was something dividing her
from the rest.

For she did not have a heart of
stone, but rather a burning flame
on her chest.

The Savages stood in wonder, for perhaps a
minute or two. It didn't take too long,
however, for the chaos to ensue.

"A Volcano Girl! A Volcano Girl!",
yelled a young Savage aloud.

The elders gathered immediately, separating
from the crowd. Everyone pointed panicked
fingers, passing along the blame;

Assuming that their cold actions were the reason that she came.

As Volcano Girl tiptoed down, each
child dropped their jaw;

Full of fear, curiosity, wonder, in awe.

When she arrived before the children, she hugged them one by one.
Suddenly, their cold hearts of
stone filled with the
warmth of a
Summer sun.

The children
stopped their fighting,
and decided to play for the sake of play.
Volcano Girl smiled with all her heart, and started to lead the way.

Suddenly, sparks began to sputter, perhaps, from her heart or soul. It seemed all those hugs were starting to take their toll.

A tiny bit of flame left her with each embrace;
Yet still, she hugged each child, a small smile on her face.

The children followed along, parading down the heated hill, to the group of angry elders, who were all arguing still.

Volcano Girl started hugging, much like she had before,
but the elders took more light, for they were
frozen to the core.
Upon her final hug, she rested in the
shade; Her flaming heart was
flickering, and it slowly
began to fade.

It was clear in that moment, without a shadow of a doubt, that the heart of poor Volcano Girl had finally been burnt out.

The Savages huddled around her, together now, unified.
They knew in order to save Volcano Girl, they must work together as a tribe.

"We have to warm her heart!", Said a Savage with a shriek.
They decided then to carry her to the top of the volcano's peak.

Once reaching the volcano's top,
they quickly gathered hands.

With one mindful breath together, their hearts
started to expand.

Their warmth and the volcano's, ignited her flame again!
Hand in hand they all rejoiced in this moment of zen.
So the Savages stood all smiling around this opening

And deep inside they now understood that every heart
is capable of love.

Every legend was once a story that just needs time to grow.
Like this one about the girl who came from the volcano.

Why This Book Was Written

I was 21 when I almost died on a tennis court: the culprit Arrhythmogenic Right Ventricular Dysplasia (ARVD). If you look it up, you will see it is a rare disease; Basically, a condition where your heart grows bigger and bigger over time.

Fast forward 14 years, involving multiple ICD shocks, surgeries, and a heart that kept on growing with passion for photography, and love for my husband and two children, who make my world go round.

My color, much like Volcano girl's, quickly began to fade; Without help, my heart would soon do the same. On Easter Sunday 2019, at the age of 35, I was on top of my own "volcano" surrounded by my family, friends, medical team, ARVD family, strangers, and at the very end, my donor who gave me the gift of life...a new heart.

After a successful surgery, I ultimately found myself surrounded by my tribe. I will spend the rest of my life trying to live up to this exceptional gift of renewed life with kindness, an open mind, and above all, an open heart, just like Volcano girl!

I found out soon after my surgery that my friend, JD Wilson (whom I met in a college creative writing class) was inspired to write this amazing book and dedicate it to me!

Johns Hopkins Heart and Vascular Institute
ARVD/C Program

What is ARVD/C?

Arrhythmogenic right ventricular dysplasia/cardiomyopathy (ARVD/C) is an inherited heart muscle condition in which the connections between the heart cells weaken and break. Scar tissue and fat replaces the damaged muscle and increases the risk of life-threatening arrhythmias and progressive decline in heart function. Although ARVD/C is rare, the disease is a leading cause of sudden cardiac death among young athletes because the strain of exercise is a significant factor in disease progression. As a result, we advise patients with ARVD/C against participating in vigorous exercise.

ARVD/C Program at Johns Hopkins Medicine

The Johns Hopkins Heart and Vascular Institute has the top ARVD/C Program in the country and is an international leader in the diagnosis, treatment, and research of this condition. Patients and their families travel from all over the world to Johns Hopkins to receive an accurate diagnosis, treatment, genetic counseling, and family screening. Many return on a regular basis for lifelong care. Under the direction of Dr. Hugh Calkins and Co-Director, Dr. Hari Tandri, the Hopkins ARVD/C Program has three objectives:

- Educate patients and physicians about ARVD/C

- Provide the latest evidence-based care to patients with known or suspected ARVD/C

- Drive the field of ARVD/C research to learn more about this condition, optimize patient quality of life, and ultimately work towards a cure

Your Support Can Make a Difference

In spite of the international reputation of the Johns Hopkins ARVD/C Program, it is extremely challenging to acquire funding for this work. As a rare disease, large grants from public sources like the NIH and the American Heart Association are few and far between making private philanthropy all the more vital to our success. **We hope you will consider partnering with us as we seek new and improved treatments for our patients and, ultimately, a cure for ARVD/C. Your donation to our efforts will truly make a difference.**

Contact: Adrienne Rose, Sr. Associate Director of Development
Johns Hopkins Heart and Vascular Institute
600 North Wolfe Street, Blalock 536B
Baltimore, MD 21287
(443)-287-7382, arose25@jhmi.edu

Online gifts: https://secure.jhu.edu/form/heart

About the author

JD is a renaissance man, a veteran, a philanthropist, a creator, a visionary, an artist, an actor, playwright, director, screenwriter, a teacher, a leader, a lover of the ocean, a friend and now a children's book author! After four years of military service and four more as an elementary school teacher, JD founded Lead U.

JD would like to give a shoutout to his parents Peter and Diane Wilson for helping this beach boy grow up to be the man he is today. Learn more about JD and Lead U below!

www.leaduthere.com
Instagram / Twitter: @lead_u_
Lead U YouTube

About the Illustrator

Ethan Roffler is a professional illustrator who loves children's books! He believes creativity and imagination are the stepping stones that can take you anywhere you want to go. He'll always remain a child at heart and has an unparalleled love for hedgehogs, puppies, and baby guinea pigs!

"I don't know
Where I've been
But I know
Where I'm going
To that volcano..."

-Beck

Made in the USA
Monee, IL
01 February 2020